Enid Blyton's

COUNTRY TALES

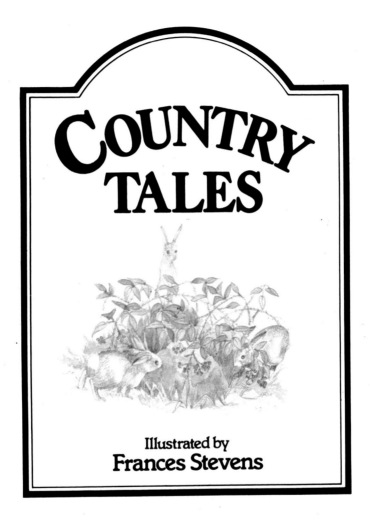

Illustrated by
Frances Stevens

AWARD PUBLICATIONS LIMITED
LONDON

ISBN 0-86163-454-3

Text copyright © 1935 Darrell Waters Limited
Illustrations copyright © 1987 Templar Publishing

This edition first published 1986 by Hutchinson Children's Books

Published 1991 by Award Publications Limited,
Spring House, Spring Place, Kentish Town,
London NW5 3BH

Printed in Hungary

CONTENTS

THE
LITTLE FAWN

For days the sun had shone from a cloudless sky, and the oak-leaves hung dry and dusty on the tree. The poppies flaunted their red frocks at the field-side, throwing off their tight green caps in the early morning, and flinging down their red petals at night, as if they really were too hot to wear anything at all. Butterflies of all kinds came to the pink and white bramble flowers on the hedgerow, and wasps and bees hummed from dawn to dusk.

The hedgerow was thirsty. The grass beneath was parched and brown. Everything wanted the cool rain. The pond water fell lower and lower, and the fish began to be anxious. What would happen if they had no water to swim in? The moorhens talked of going to the big river, but they were fond of the little pond and stayed.

And then, late one afternoon the rain came. Great purple-black clouds sailed up from the south-west and covered all the sky. It seemed very dark after the brilliance of the summer sun. Then suddenly a flash of bright lightning tore the sky in half, and the startled birds flew to the hedge for shelter. Almost at once there came a loud peal of thunder that rolled round the sky, and sent the young rabbits scampering back to their burrows in fright.

And then, what a downpour! First came big drops that made wide round ripples on the pond, and set the oak-tree leaves dancing up and down. Then came a deluge of smaller drops, beating down faster and faster. The old toad crawled out from his stone and lay in the rainstorm, his mouth opening and shutting in delight as he felt the rain trickling down his back. Crowds of young frogs jumped out of the pond and hopped to the ditch for joy. The hedge-hog found a sheltered place and curled up in disgust, for he didn't like the way the rain ran down his prickles. It tickled him.

Soon a delicious smell arose from the field and hedge – the smell of the rain sinking into the earth. All the animals sniffed it. It was good. In their ears sounded the rippling and gurgling, the splashing and the dripping of the rain. They heard every plant drinking greedily. They heard the excited moorhens scuttling in the rain over the pond. It was a glorious time.

The clouds grew blacker. The lightning flashed again and the thunder growled and grumbled like a great bear in the sky – and just as the storm was at its height there came the sound of tiny galloping hooves. They sounded through the pattering of the rain, and all the rabbits heard them and peeped out of their holes, the rain wetting their fine whiskers. The toad heard them too and crawled back to his hole. He did not wish to be trampled on.

The newcomer ran to the hedgerow and stopped there in its shelter. It was a small fawn, a baby deer, only a few weeks old. The hedgerow was surprised, for it had never seen a fawn before.

The little fawn was trembling. Its soft eyes were wide with fright, and its tail swung to and fro. Another peal of thunder sounded overhead, beginning with a noise like a giant clapping of hands. The fawn closed its eyes in terror and sank down on the grass.

It was frightened of the storm. Its mother had left it safely hidden in the bracken of the distant wood, and had told it to stay there until she returned. But then the storm had come, and the little fawn, who had never seen lightning before, or heard thunder, had been terrified. The jays in the wood had screamed in delight at the rain, and the fawn had thought they were screeching in terror. Fear had filled his small, beating heart and he had run from his hiding-place, through the wood, across the fields – anywhere, anywhere, to get away from this dreadful noise and terrible flashing light.

But the storm seemed to follow him. The rain came and lashed him, beating into his eyes. The thunder rolled exactly above his head – or so it seemed to him. Where was his mother? Why did she not come to him? He was so frightened that his legs would no longer carry him and he sank down on the grass beside the old hedgerow.

He made a little bleating sound and the old mother rabbit, who had heard many young animals crying for their mother, looked out of a hole nearby. She saw the frightened fawn and was sorry for him. She ran out of her burrow in the rain and went up to the panting fawn.

'Don't be afraid,' she said. 'It is only a thunderstorm. It will pass. Be glad of the good rain, little creature, and lick it from the grass. It will taste good.'

The fawn looked at the soft-eyed rabbit and was comforted. It was good to see another creature near him – one that was not frightened. He put out his hot tongue and licked the wet grass.

The raindrops were cool and sweet. He stopped trembling and lay calmly in the rain.

'Come under the hedgerow,' said the rabbit. 'You will get wet lying there. This hedgerow is thick and will shelter you well till the storm is past.'

The little fawn obediently pushed his way into the hedge and lay down in the dry, though he could easily reach the dripping grass with his pink tongue.

'Where do you come from?' asked the rabbit, inquisitively. 'I have never seen you before, though I have heard my mother tell of creatures like you in the woods.'

'I am a young fallow deer,' said the fawn, looking at the rabbit out of his beautiful big eyes. 'I was born this summer. I live in the wood with my mother, and I have a fine hiding-place there among the high bracken.'

'Bracken is good for hiding in,' said the rabbit. 'Where are your antlers, little fawn? I thought deer had antlers on their heads.'

'I have none yet,' said the fawn. 'But next year they will begin to grow. They will look like two horns at first, but in the second year they will grow more like antlers and every year they will grow bigger and bigger, until I am fully-grown and have great antlers like those on my father's head.'

'Surely those big antlers are a nuisance to you?' said the rabbit, in surprise. 'Don't they catch in the tree branches as you run?'

'No,' said the fawn. 'We throw our heads backwards as we run, and then our antlers lie along our sides and do not catch anything. Also they protect our bodies from any scratches or bruises we might get as we run through the trees and bushes. My mother has no antlers – but I shall grow some soon.'

'Do you wear them all the year round?' asked the rabbit.

'Oh, no,' said the fawn. 'They drop off in the springtime and then grow again in a few weeks. On my head I have two little bumps, and it is from these I shall grow my antlers each year. My father has wonderful antlers, very large and spreading, and they show what a great age he is. But he will drop his antlers next springtime, and they will have to grow again from the knobs on his forehead. That is what my mother told me.'

'How strange!' said the rabbit, looking at the little dappled fawn as he lay under the hedge. 'What do you eat, little creature?'

'Oh, I eat grass and toadstools and the shoots of young trees,' said the fawn, beginning to feel hungry. 'And often we eat the bark of trees. I should like something to eat now.'

'There are some turnips in the field on the other side of the hedge,' said the rabbit. 'Would you like some?'

The fawn did not know what turnips were, but he jumped to his feet and followed the rabbit, squeezing himself through the hedge.   The storm was over now, but the rain still fell gently. The thunder was muttering far away over the hills, but there was no longer any lightning. Blue sky began to appear between the ragged clouds and once the sun peeped through.

All the hedgerow was hung with twinkling raindrops. The oak-tree shone brilliantly, for every one of its leaves had been well washed by the rain. The fawn slipped into the turnip field and began to nibble at the young turnips. They were delicious.

When he had eaten enough he went back to the hedgerow. The rabbit followed him and told him that he should go back to the woods, for his mother would be anxious about him – but at that very moment the blackbird in the tree above sent out his alarm cry.

'Kukka-kuk! Beware! Here comes a strange enemy!'

Every animal scuttled back to its hole, and all the birds flew to the topmost branches. The little fawn stood up and smelt the air. Suddenly he made a strange, welcoming sound and rushed up to the newcomer. It was his mother, a big, well-grown deer, with soft eyes and small, neat feet with cloven hooves.

She nuzzled her fawn in delight. She had missed him from his hiding-place and had come to seek him.

'Come,' she said to him. 'You should not have run away, little fawn. Enemies might have seen you and captured you. You are safe under the bracken in the woods.'

'But a loud and flashing enemy came,' said the fawn, rubbing himself against his mother lovingly. 'I was afraid.'

'That was only a storm,' said his mother.

'There are good turnips in the field over there,' said the little fawn. 'I have eaten some.'

'We will stay under this hedge until the dark comes,' said the deer. 'Then we will feast on the turnips before we return to the woods. Let us find a dry place.'

Under the thick ivy was a big, dry patch, for the ivy leaves made a dense shelter there. The deer lay down with her fawn beside her and they waited until evening came. They lay so quiet that none of the hedgerow folk feared them, and little mice, the hedgehog and the toad went about their business just as usual.

After they had fed on the sweet turnips the little fawn called goodbye to the old rabbit who had been so kind, and then in the soft blue evening time the two trotted back to the woodlands.

'Come again!' called the rabbits, who liked the gentle deer. 'Come again and share our turnips!'

THE END

DOZYMOUSE
AND FLITTERMOUSE

The little dormouse knew the hedgerow from end to end. He had lived there for two summers and winters, and he knew every creature that ran beneath the hedge, perched in the bushes, or flew in the air above. His big black eyes watched everything.

He was a small, tawny-coloured mouse, with a long, thickly-furred tail. He could run and he could climb, and even the oak-tree knew him well, for he had many times run up the trunk and along the branches to talk to the squirrel there.

At first the red squirrel had thought the dormouse was a tiny squirrel, for he had such a furry tail, such large bright eyes, and the squirrel-like habit of sitting upright with a nut in his paws.

'A squirrel!' said the dormouse in surprise. 'No, not I! I'm one of the mouse family. I've lots of names – dormouse is my right name, but I'm often called Sleepymouse and sometimes Dozymouse. I sleep very soundly, you know.'

'Well, I know a queer creature called Flittermouse,' said the red squirrel. 'You must be a cousin of his.'

'I've never head of him,' said the dormouse. 'Where does he live?'

'He lives inside the oak-tree,' said the squirrel. 'Come and peep.'

The dormouse looked into the hollow trunk of the old oak-tree. He saw something black there, hanging upside down, perfectly still.

'Why,' he said, 'it's a bat! I thought you said it was a flittermouse.'

'Well, so it is, isn't it?' said the squirrel. 'It's like a little brown mouse with big black wings that flit about in the dusk – a flittermouse.'

The dormouse woke up the bat. It stretched itself and unfolded its webby wings. It had hung itself up by its hook-like thumbs.

'Is it night-time?' asked the bat in a thin, squeaky voice. 'Are there many flies and beetles about?'

'It is indeed getting dark,' answered the dormouse. 'But, please tell me something. The squirrel says you must be a cousin of mine. But how can you be a mouse if you have wings? You must be a bird.'

'No, no,' said the bat, flying out of the tree and perching very awkwardly beside the dormouse. 'I am no bird. Look at me. I haven't a feather on my back. I don't lay eggs, either.'

'What are your wings made of, then?' asked the dormouse.

'Look!' said the bat, and he stretched out one of his strange wings. 'The bones of my fingers have grown enormously long, and I have grown black skin over them to make wings. Isn't it a good idea?'

'I wish *I* could do that,' said the dormouse. 'How do you grow your fingers so long?'

But he received no answer for the bat was off and away into the air, darting here and there easily and swiftly. He caught some evening beetles and popped each one into a little pouch he had by his tail. Then he feasted on them, giving high little squeaks of delight as he flew.

The dormouse watched him in envy. He liked flies when he could catch them, though he found it better to feed on nuts or grain, for fly-food darted away, and nuts and grain kept still. He peeped inside the oak-tree where the bat had hidden. It smelt strongly of bat.

'I'm glad I don't smell like that,' he said to himself, as he ran quickly down the tree. He stopped at the bottom, and sniffed in every direction. He was always on the look-out for weasels, who loved a feast of dormouse.

There was no enemy near, so the dormouse ran to his summer nest to tell his wife to come out and hunt. He went to the hedgerow and clambered up the brambles. A little way up was his nest, in which he had had several families of tiny dormice that summer. Now the last of them had gone, and all were running about on their own. The dormouse sometimes met them in the hedgerow, but most of them had grown so big that he hardly knew them.

The nest was well made, tucked into the bramble stems. The dormouse had decided to make it of the bark from the stems of the old honeysuckle that grew farther down the hedgerow. He had torn it off in long strips, and he and his wife had made their nest with the pieces. Inside they had lined the nest with leaves, so that it was cosy and warm. It was so well hidden that not even the rabbits guessed where it was.

In the daytime the dormice hid in their nest and slept soundly. At night they woke up and went hunting for food. They loved nuts, berries and grain, and if they chanced upon a fat caterpillar they would take that too. As the summer went by they grew fatter and fatter, and the nest shook with their weight!

'When the autumn comes we must build a nest underground,' said the dormice. 'This one will be too easily seen when the bramble leaves fall.'

When October came the dormice were so fat and round that there really was not enough room for them both in their nest. The nights became chilly. The dormice felt more and more sleepy.

So they hunted about and at last found a little tunnel going right down among the roots of the hedgerow, quite a long way underground. They took some moss down the hole and arranged it in a little round place among the roots. They would be warm and comfortable there, far away from any enemy.

'Now we must take plenty of food down to our new nest,' said the dormouse to his wife. 'We might wake up on a warm winter's day and feel hungry.'

It was while they were hunting for food that they heard the bat calling to them. The dormouse once again climbed the oak-tree and looked at the queer little bat clinging clumsily to the branch.

'I want to say goodbye,' said the bat. 'It's getting cold now, and I am going to hide myself away for the winter.'

'We are just doing the same!' said the dormouse in surprise. 'We have made a nice nest far underground among the hedgerow roots, and we are hoarding up some food in case we wake up on a warm winter's day and want a meal.'

'I don't do that,' said the bat. My food wouldn't keep like yours. It would go bad, because I eat only beetles and flies. But if I wake up it will be such a warm spell that a few flies are sure to be about, too, and I shall catch them. I am going to fly to an old cave I know across the fields. A great many of my relations will be there – big bats and little bats, long-eared bats and short-eared ones, and little common bats like myself.'

'Do you make a nest?' asked the dormouse.

'Of course not!' said the bat. 'No bat ever makes a nest! We shall all hang ourselves up by our hooked thumbs, upside down, cover ourselves with our wings and soon we will be fast asleep.'

'What do you do with your young ones if you don't make a nest to keep them in?' asked the dormouse in surprise.

'Oh, we keep our little ones cuddled against our fur, even when we fly in the air,' answered the bat. 'They cling tightly and never fall. Well, dormouse, I hope I see you well and fat in the springtime. You look fat enough now!'

'So do you!' said the little dormouse.

'Ah, it's a good thing to get fat before the long, hungry wintertime!' said the bat. 'We shall get through the cold days comfortably then. Well, goodbye.'

'Just come and see my nest before you go,' begged the dormouse.

'I can't,' said the bat, impatiently. 'Haven't you seen my knees? They turn backwards instead of forwards, so that I can't walk. I am only made for flying!' He rose into the air and darted swiftly away.

'Goodbye, little flittermouse!' called the dormouse, and then, feeling a touch of frost in the air, he ran quickly to his hole. His small fat wife was waiting for him. Without a word they curled up together in the warm moss and fell asleep. They became as cold as ice, they seemed not to breathe, so soundly asleep were they – but a warm night would awaken them, and then they would feast eagerly on their little store of nuts in the roots of the hedgerow.

THE END

THE
GREY MINER

The hedgerow stood bare and cold in the November sunshine. The frost had stripped the last few leaves from the hawthorn, hazel and brambles, and only the ivy was green. The oak-tree that spread its big branches overhead still had some rustling brown leaves left, and these shone like old copper in the sun.

The leaves from the hedgerow lay in dry heaps in the ditch below. They crackled when any creature trod on them. Their bright colours had faded to a dull brown; the little creatures of the hedgerow found them useful for nest-linings, for the dry leaves were cosy and warm to sleep in.

There were not many hedgerow folk about now. It was too cold. The dormice were fast asleep. The lizards and newts were hidden safely away, and the bat had hung himself upside down in a nearby cave. It was wintertime.

But there was one little creature who was still very busy on this sunshiny November day. He did not go to sleep for the winter as some of the hedgerow creatures did, because he was always too hungry to sleep for long. He was a little grey mole, the miner of the hedgerow.

He lived so much underground that his eyes were almost no use to him, they had become so deeply buried in his velvety fur. But he had little use for eyes – it was his nose and his ears that helped him to find his food!

All through the summer days he had hunted for worms, grubs, slugs and beetles. He had gone down the underground runs that had been used by hundreds of moles before – long, straight runs worn smooth and round by the passing of many velvety bodies. From these runs the mole had tunnelled sideways in search of worms, throwing up the earth as he went, making many little molehills that showed the way he had gone.

Now that the winter had come there were fewer creatures about, and sometimes many days passed before the mole met any one on his journeys, except little grey miners like himself. Today he was frightened, for a strange thing had happened. He had had a nest deep in a molehill on the other side of the field, not far from a little brook. For four days the rain had fallen without stopping, and at the end of the fourth day the brook had overflowed its banks. The water had flooded the mole's tunnel and had poured into his nest.

In a great fright, the little creature began to tunnel upwards, and at last came up into the open air on the very top of his molehill. Water was all around him – only the height of his hill saved him from the flood.

Soon the water went down a little, and the mole stepped into it. He did not dare to tunnel downwards, for he was afraid of being caught by the water below ground. He found that the water round his hill was deep, but he could swim well; so away he went, striking out with his spade-like front paws as fast as he could.

Soon he came to the end of the water. He was on the earth again. He burrowed downwards, throwing out the soil with his paws, and at last struck a tunnel, one of the many that ran across the field. He went along it and reached the hedgerow, which he knew quite well. There was a fine straight run that ran all along the hedgerow. It was dry and felt warm. The mole made up his mind to make a new nest under the hedge, so he began to make a side tunnel towards the hedgerow.

His sharp nose smelt a worm as he worked. At once he thrust his strong snout into the earth and dug swiftly with his clawed feet. In a trice he reached the worm, which lay coiled up cosily in its small chamber of earth, and he gobbled it up greedily. Then he went on with his tunnelling.

Now just nearby was a fine hole used by a hedgehog for her winter sleep. She lay curled up there, dry and warm. When the back wall of her hole gave way and the mole appeared behind her, the hedgehog woke up in a fright. She at once thought it was an enemy, and curled herself up all the more tightly.

'Move yourself,' said the mole, pushing up against the frightened hedgehog. He had a high, squeaky voice like a bat. 'I am tunnelling here.'

The hedgehog knew the mole's voice, and uncurled at once.

'Why do you disturb me?' she asked, angrily. 'I was fast asleep. You should sleep, too, in this cold weather.'

'I wish I could,' said the mole. 'But I am always too hungry. Do you know whether there are many grubs about under this hedgerow? I should like to find some of those fat grey leather-jackets; they make a fine meal, and I am very hungry.'

The hedgehog looked at the mole's velvety coat, so different from her own mass of spines.

'You will find plenty of worms and grubs in this bank,' she said. 'Tell me, how do you manage to keep your coat so clean and tidy, living underground as you do, tunnelling all day long?'

'It's easy,' said the mole. 'My coat is very short and all the hairs stand straight up – they do not lie backwards like the rabbit's. So it doesn't really matter if I go forwards or backwards in my tunnels – the hairs will bend either way quite easily. Why don't you tunnel, too? You have a long snout, like mine, and could easily burrow with it.'

'No, I couldn't,' said the hedgehog. 'I use it for turning over leaves when I look for slugs, but it isn't strong like yours. I have seen you thrusting your snout into the earth and throwing it up easily. May I see your paws? I have often wanted to see how it is you can dig so well.'

The mole held out a front hand. It was very curious, for the palm was turned outwards, instead of inwards. It was very broad, and the nails were large and strong. The mole could not close his hand; he always had to hold it open. It was immensely strong, exactly the right shape for digging and tunnelling.

'I shall have my nest under this hedgerow,' said the mole. 'It seems a good place. I can smell plenty of worms about.'

'How do you build your nest?' asked the hedgehog, sleepily. 'I just find a hole and line it with leaves and moss.'

'Oh, I shall tunnel until I am right under the hedge,' answered the mole. 'Then I shall make a nice hole there, throwing up the earth above it till there is quite a big hill. I expect I shall have to make one or two tunnels through the hill to throw out all the earth. If I feel cold I shall line my hole with a few leaves, as you have done. It will be my resting-place, and when I am not there I shall be hunting all around under the ground for grubs and worms.'

'Don't eat them all,' begged the hedgehog. 'I might go hunting myself on a warm winter's night.'

'Tell me when you do, and I'll take you to the best hunting-ground,' promised the mole.

'Will you have any children living with you in your nest?' asked the hedgehog, remembering how she had had seven little hedgehogs with her in the summertime.

27

'Oh no,' said the mole. 'I never have them in *my* nest. I had a
wife who made a very big nest for our young ones this summer. It
was out in the middle of the field, though I warned her it was not a
good place. She took leaves and grasses to her hole in her mouth,
to make the nest nice and soft. I saw the young moles.
They were queer, wrinkled little creatures.
But before they could look after
themselves a dog came and
smelt them out.

He destroyed the
nest-hill and found the
little ones. My wife escaped
down the tunnel, but she
was so frightened that she
fled to another field.'
'A badger ate one of *my*
little ones,' said the hedgehog,
suddenly remembering her poor
youngster. 'But all the rest are grown up
and have found holes of their own to sleep in. I don't think I
should know them now if I met them. You had better go now,
mole. I want to sleep again.'

The hedgehog curled herself up tightly and in a few minutes
was snoring softly. The mole turned and went back into his
tunnel. He dug hard for a few minutes, ate three worms and a
grub, and then found himself just underneath the thickest part of
the hedgerow, where he planned to make his nest.

He began to loosen the earth with his strong, spadelike paws.
He pushed it upwards with his snout. As the hole became big, so

the hill above grew big, too, for all the earth from the hole was thrown there. Soon the mole had to take the earth right up through the hill, and to do that he had to tunnel up it. But it was not long before he had the inner hole big enough to satisfy himself. He settled down in it comfortably to have a short sleep, for he was tired. His hill rose up under the brambles in the hedgerow and was well hidden.

He fell asleep and dreamed of all the things he liked so much to eat. The rabbits came out from their hole and looked at the new mound of earth in the hedgerow.

'A mole has come to live here,' they said. 'We shall sometimes meet him where his tunnels cross our burrows. Our hedgerow will shelter yet one more creature this winter!'

The oak-tree rustled loudly. It would feel yet another patter of feet over its deep and tangled roots, and it was glad.

THE END

NEVER SAY DIE!

All day long and all night long, too, there was a coming and going in the hedgerow. Rabbits and voles, mice and rats, birds of all kinds went to and fro about their business, squeaking, chirping, chattering. Usually the hedgerow folk were happy and contented, but sometimes there came a great outcry and disturbance when a hated enemy came slinking by or flew down from overhead.

'Stoat!' would come the signal from a wary rabbit, and at once all the hedgerow folk would vanish. 'Sparrowhawk!' was another cry, feared by the many chirruping sparrows. 'Owl!' would squeak a terrified mouse at night, peeping from his hole to see a shadowy wing passing overhead.

The blackbird was a good friend to all the little creatures in the hedgerow. He often sat high up on the oak-tree to sing his beautiful, flute-like song, and from his high branch he could see many things. He could see the brown, slinking stoat, and he could spy the smaller weasel, gliding like a snake along the ditch.

As soon as he saw them, he would give
the alarm, and his loud, harsh cries would go
ringing up the hedgerow and down, striking
fear into every small, beating heart.
Mice, rabbits, voles, birds – they would all
take flight, silently and fearfully.

The cunning stoat or sly weasel would
stay still by a tuft of grass, hating the blackbird,
whose sharp eyes had seen them gliding along.
But the blackbird, safe in the tree, cared nothing and,
as long as he saw the enemy below, he continued to send
out his alarm-call, warning all the furred and feathered folk to
keep under cover.

But for a long time no weasel or stoat had come to the
hedgerow, and life had been peaceful. The owl had come two or
three times at night, and the sparrowhawk had flashed round the
hedge after a frightened chaffinch one late afternoon – but there
had been nothing very frightening besides these two happenings.

For the last two or three weeks something strange had come
to the hedgerow – something that puzzled the little folk very
much. Soft white flakes had fallen from the sky, and the fields all
around were covered with a white blanket, cold and soft to tiny
paws. The weather had turned cold again, and the snow had
come to pile up in drifts here and there, and to cover every tree
and bush with white.

The mice made narrow runs under the snow. The rabbits came out and tried to find grass beneath it, but they were half-scared at the strange, white glare of the fields. Some of them went to nibble at the bark of the ivy, for they were very hungry. The rats grew thin and fierce, and grumbled bitterly among themselves.

'We cannot get near the farmer's food store,' said one. 'There is a weasel there, and he kills every rat that ventures near.'

'The mice are difficult to catch in this snow,' said another rat, showing his sharp teeth. 'They would be good to eat, for they are fat with feasting on their stores of hidden seeds.'

The rats were crouching in the snowy ditch, sniffing at a pile of dry little bones, which had once belonged to a thrush, killed in the autumn. Only the bones were left now, and the rats knew there was no joy to be had from eating them. One of the rats was weak with hunger, and a fierce-looking companion was eyeing it, wondering if he could fight it and kill it. Just as he was about to spring on his companion, a whisper went through the hedgerow.

'Stoat! Stoat!'

· Never Say Die! ·

The rats scattered and vanished – all but the one who had been about to spring on his weak companion. The stoat had come silently behind him and sprung swiftly. The rat lay on his side, bitten deeply in the neck. He was dead.

The stoat looked round him and sniffed. He was in the ditch, and the snow there was much trodden by little feet.

He could smell mice, too, and the little pile of thrush bones. And he could smell rabbit.

Rabbit! The stoat was lean and hungry, for hunting had been bad. He longed for a meal of rabbit – but, meanwhile, here was the dead rat, and that would do for a starving stoat.

He could hardly be seen against the snow, for he was pure white all over, save for a black tip to his tail. His eyes were dark and fierce, and he stared steadily around him as he feasted on the rat. Suddenly he pricked up his ears. He could hear sounds on the other side of the hedge – a frightened squeak and a flurry of snow.

The stoat shot up the side of the ditch and leapt up the bank. He saw a hole in the hedge and ran to it.

At the very same moment a brown creature arrived at the hole from the other side, and the two met, nose to nose. They backed a little and glared at one another. Then they recognized each other, and flashed a greeting from their bright black eyes.

'Good-day, cousin,' said the weasel. 'You smell of a successful hunt.'

'I have killed a rat,' said the stoat. 'I heard you hunting a mouse.'

'There is not much in a mouse,' said the weasel, sniffing the rat-smell longingly, but knowing very well that he could not share the rat with the stoat. 'Times are bad, cousin.'

'Never say die!' said the stoat, going back to the dead rat. 'That

33

is our motto, cousin! Never say die! We are fierce and strong, and as long as there is an enemy to be hunted we will hunt him.'

'Cousin stoat,' said the weasel, who had been eyeing the stoat's coat with some surprise, 'how is it that you are white like the snow now? You were red-brown when I last saw you, and if it had not been for your large, bright eyes and your stoat-smell I would not have known you.'

'My coat has turned white since the snow came,' answered the stoat. 'How can I hunt well if my coat is brown when the snow is so white? I should be too easily seen. So my coat has changed, and only the tip of my tail has stayed black. I shall change back again to my usual red-brown when the warm weather comes.'

'It is a strange thing, but most useful,' said the weasel. 'You are lucky, cousin. You are larger than I am, to begin with, which makes you a more dangerous enemy, and now that you are white you are most difficult to see! I am glad I am not your enemy!'

'That is all very well, but I should like a good meal of young rabbit,' said the stoat, 'and, despite my coat, they are hard to catch. They do not come out so much now that the snow is here.'

'I have tried my best to catch a rabbit,' said the weasel, 'but I am too easily seen now. My coat shows up so plainly in the snow. Wait, though! I may be able to catch one in another way. There are plenty of rabbits in this hedgerow, I know. I once had a nest here with my wife, and we saw hundreds of rabbits about these fields. When she took our little ones out to teach them hunting they had plenty to eat. Would you like to see me catch a rabbit without chasing it, cousin?'

'Yes,' said the stoat, who was now well fed and quite agreeable to lying down in the snow and watching someone else hunt.

'Then watch me,' said the small weasel, his short tail quivering with excitement and his large black eyes fierce with hunger. He glided down to the ditch and then up the side of it into the field. The stoat watched him.

The weasel sat in the snow for a moment, quite silent. He could see a few rabbits watching him from their holes, ready to bolt at once if he came near. Then he began to do the most extraordinary things, quite amazing to watch.

First, he squirmed from side to side. He threw himself up in the air and down. He leapt sideways, then he turned himself round and round and round. He flung himself over and rolled on his back, and then he sprang the right way up and bounded round in a circle. The watching rabbits could hardly believe their eyes. What was happening to this weasel? *Could* it be a weasel if it behaved so queerly? They had never seen anything so strange before.

Three rabbits came right out of their holes to watch more closely. A small mouse looked out from his little burrow. A dozen sparrows sat chattering in the trees, astonished at the sight of the weasel behaving as if he were completely mad. The blackbird flew up, too, and looked to see what was happening. He saw the weasel and was just about to utter his cry of alarm to warn everyone else, when he found that the weasel was rolling over and over on the ground. Was he hurt? Why was he behaving like this? Now look at him, jumping up in the air as if he were mad! The blackbird was amazed, and forgot to utter his alarm-cry.

One of the rabbits, a young one, only born the summer before, moved closer to the strange weasel. He was fascinated, puzzled, amazed. The weasel watched him from unblinking black eyes. And then a memory came into the mind of the blackbird on the bough. He had seen this before!

'It's a trick!' cried the blackbird in his ringing voice. 'It's a trick! Beware, you rabbits! Run, mouse! It's a trick, I tell you! He'll catch you! He'll catch you!'

The mouse disappeared. Two of the rabbits
bolted. The sparrows flew to the top of
the oak-tree, chirruping in terror. Only the
young rabbit remained, and he seemed not to
hear what the blackbird said. The weasel heard, and his
bright eyes flashed in hate at the blackbird who was spoiling
his sport. He ran round and round in a narrow circle,
whilst the rabbit sat and watched
him, his nose trembling in
delight at the
astonishing
scene.

The weasel widened his circle a little, and the watching stoat,
hidden in the ditch, stiffened. He knew quite well that the weasel
was going to strike very soon now. All the hairs rose on his back
and his tail swelled.

Almost at once the weasel darted at the rabbit, flung himself on
the startled creature's neck and gave him the death-bite. The
rabbit gave a pitiful squeak and died. The stoat came out from his
hiding-place and eyed the feast, not daring to join in, for he
feared the savage little weasel.

'Never say die!' said the starving weasel in triumph. 'If one trick
doesn't serve, another will.'

'I told you so, I told you so!' cried the blackbird to the dead
rabbit.

'He was always a foolish little creature,' said the other rabbits,
hidden close in their burrow. 'It is a wonder he lived so long.
Poor, silly little rabbit!'

THE END

KEEP AWAY !

From the time when the hedgerow had first been planted until now, when it had grown high and thick, the birds had lived there. They had nested there, hunted for food among the leaves, roosted there at night, and sung from the topmost sprays when their young ones had hatched out. The hedgerow had heard many different songs and calls, and had hidden many a neatly made nest.

The little brown wren was always flitting in and out of the hedge; the quiet hedge-sparrow had for two years built her nest there, and laid inside it her pretty, sky-blue eggs; the chaffinch had once built a beautiful nest in the ivy leaves, and had trimmed it outside with lichen from the ditch beneath. But the bird that the hedgerow knew best of all was the robin redbreast.

The robin was such an inquisitive, restless little bird. Whatever happened in or under the hedgerow he had to know about. If a hedgehog came shuffling by, the robin flitted about above him in the hedge. If a weasel glided silently along in the ditch below, the robin set up a loud tick-tick-tick sound and warned every other creature in the hedgerow so that they fled for shelter. He was always about, from dawn to dusk, and was the last to go to roost.

In the springtime two or three robins could be found in the hedgerow, but when winter came only one sang his creamy little song there. He lived there, and rarely left the hedge and its surrounding piece of meadow. He hunted for worms in the grass, and rooted about for insects in the moist ditch. There were not very many for him to find, so he became rather thin – but he didn't *look* thin, because the cold weather made him fluff out his feathers and look twice as big as he really was!

One day another robin flew down to the hedgerow and looked around. He was a handsome fellow, bold and lively. His bright eyes flashed, and he flicked his wings and bobbed his tail up and down. Then he gave a rich little trill.

The other robin, who had lived in the hedge all the autumn and part of the winter, heard the song at once and answered it defiantly.

'How dare you come to my hedge?' he sang. 'This is my piece of ground. Keep away! Keep away!'

'It is a nice hedge!' sang back the second robin. 'I will have it for my own.'

Two bullfinches poked their heads out from the ivy, where they had been sitting side by side. They felt sure there was going to be a fight. That would make the fifth fight this winter between the robins.

'Quarrelsome creatures!' said the cock bullfinch, fluffing out his brick-red chest. 'Why can't they live in peace with one another, as you and I do all the year round, little wife?'

The two robins were now shouting their war-song so loudly that a horde of inquisitive sparrows flew up to see what was the matter. 'Cheer-up, cheer-up, cheer-up!' they cried, excitedly.

'This is my hedge, I tell you!' sang the first robin. 'Keep away from it, or I will fight you!'

'Then fight me, for I say it is *my* hedge!' sang the second robin. With that the two small birds flung themselves at one another, still singing loudly, and began to fight. How they pecked! How they struck with their quivering wings! And how they sang! It was marvellous to hear. The sparrows were immensely excited, and cheered loudly. Only the two bullfinches were disgusted.

The hen bullfinch peered out again and gave a little cry of horror.

'Will you believe it! The second robin is the hedgerow robin's *son*! Yes, he is. I know him by a tiny white feather in one wing. To think that a robin should fight his father, and a father his son!'

· Keep Away! ·

The bullfinches chattered together, and rubbed their cone-shaped beaks lovingly, one against the other. They were affectionate birds, and had lived together for five years, building a nest each year and helping one another always.

They remembered quite well how happy the robin had been that spring when he and his lively little wife had come hunting for a nesting-place in the hedgerow. The cock-bird had wanted to nest low down in the hedge, and they had almost decided on a spot when the hen robin gave a wild trill of joy.

'Look! Here is an old boot thrown in the ditch!' she sang. 'Let us build there! I love to build my nest in something that humans have used. Last year my nest was in an old kettle, and the year before I built it in a tin.'

'I was brought up in an old saucepan,' said her mate. 'Last year *I* had a nest in a watering-can in the garden of a house. I like humans. They are kind and friendly. They throw out crumbs for us, and when they work in their gardens they dig up grubs for us to eat. They are nice creatures. I would dearly love to build our nest in something they have used. Let us look at the old boot.'

So they hopped down to the ditch and examined the dirty, gaping old boot. It was just what they wanted. How pleased they were! How they sang about it! The two bullfinches, who had just decided to build their nest in the hedge above, thought that the two robins were mad to choose such a queer place when they could have chosen a nice, cosy home in the hedge.

The robins made a big, bulky nest inside the boot. They used the old brown oak leaves in the ditch, and some soft moss. They lined the nest with cow-hairs and three chicken feathers they had found at the farm across the fields. Then the hen laid four pretty eggs mottled with light red, and the two birds were as happy as the day was long.

The bullfinches had been happy, too. Their nest was quite different. It was a frail little platform of sticks, very cunningly woven. On it the bullfinches had placed a cup-like arrangement of roots, and inside they had neatly lined it with sheep-hairs and cow-hairs. The hen had laid five beautiful eggs, a dark green-blue, streaked with purple and red. The young robins and bullfinches had hatched out at exactly the same time, and the hen-birds had been most interested in each other's nestlings. They had often gone to peep into one another's nest.

The cock robin was so proud of his brood of nestlings that he had sung about them loudly whenever he had a moment to spare, which was not often, for they were very hungry little creatures. The hen loved them, too, and when the weasel had come slipping by she had been almost mad with fear. But all the nestlings had been reared safely, and the robins had had a second family in the old boot.

Then the bullfinches had seen a most extraordinary thing. When autumn came the little hen had wanted to live in the hedgerow, but the cock robin had driven her angrily away. The two bullfinches had watched in horror. They lived joyfully together all the year round, and they could not understand such ways. Now here was the cock robin fighting again – this time with his own son.

'I shall go and stop them,' said the cock bullfinch at last. 'They are making such a noise that the sparrowhawk will hear and come swooping down on us.'

He flew to where the two robins were fighting. Just as he got there the old robin gave the young one such a vicious peck that

he fell to the ground. As soon as he touched the grass he was up again, and flew over the hedge and away to the wood as fast as he could, quite defeated.

'Keep away, keep away!' trilled the old robin. 'This is *my* hedgerow.'

'You should be ashamed to fight your own family,' said the bullfinch. 'I never fight *my* family.'

'Oh, you!' said the robin, scornfully. 'You don't need to! You can feed on all kinds of things that are easy to find in the wintertime – seeds, berries, winter-buds. But we robins are different. We feed on insects, and they are very difficult to get in the winter. One hedgerow, bank and ditch will only feed one robin – so we each have our own patch in winter and must keep to it. That son of mine I fought just now ought to know better than to come here! This hedgerow is mine! I tell you, all robins must have their own little piece of ground in winter or starve! It is a wise rule. This is my hedgerow, I say!'

The bullfinch flew off. He thought there was something in what the robin had said – or rather sang, for all of his long speech had been trilled at the top of his liquid voice. After all, insects *were* very scarce in the winter. If three or four robins all lived in the same place they would certainly starve to death.

'What did he say to you?' asked the hen bullfinch.

'He told me why he fought,' said the bullfinch. 'I think he is right, after all. Robins must fight in the winter, but bullfinches need not. Shall we go and find some dock-seeds?'

So the two happy birds flew off – and as they went they heard the robin singing at the top of his lovely voice. 'Keep away! Keep away! This is my hedgerow! Keep away!'

THE END

THE
BLUE VISITOR

The pond that lay quietly near the hedgerow was always a very busy place. The frogs croaked there, and newts swam about in the water. Wild ducks sometimes came, and the slow-flying heron, with his deep voice calling 'Kronk! Kronk!' Snakes hunted for fish in the water, swimming gracefully, and most of the birds drank from the edge. So did the hedgerow animals – some in the daytime, but most of them at night.

King of the pond was the little black moorhen, with his bobbing, red-marked head and long dark-green legs. He lived there all the year round, feeding on fish, tadpoles, water-weeds and anything else he could pick up for a living. He could often be heard clucking among the reeds, and the hedgerow folk knew him very well indeed. He could run as fast as he could swim, and sometimes he spread his wings and flew off to the farm away in the distance to have a meal of grain.

The year before he had had a nice little wife, but she had been caught by a cunning fox. So when the springtime came and the moorhen wanted a nest, there was no little mate to help him to build one.

'Where shall I find a mate?' he said to himself as he swam across the pond, bobbing his perky little head. 'The primroses are here, the sky is as blue as the little speedwell on the bank, it is springtime – but I have no one to love!'

That day a visitor came to the pond. It was a kingfisher, gleaming blue and green in the sunshine. He was rather a stumpy bird to look at, with a long strong beak, and a short tail – but his brightly coloured feathers made him beautiful! His chestnut breast shone, his back was sky blue, and his head and wings gleamed a marvellous green as he turned here and there. The moorhen gaped at him in envy. *He* was black, sober black, with the front of his head and base of his bill a bright red – a dull creature compared with the brilliance of the kingfisher!

The kingfisher was friendly. He sat on an alder branch that streched over the pond and looked for fish in the water below.

'You will find more fish if you come down and swim on the water,' said the moor-hen. 'That is how I catch *my* fish!'

'And this is how I catch *mine*!' called the kingfisher, diving into the water like an arrow. He came up with a fish wriggling in his mouth. He knocked it sharply against the alder branch and killed it. Then he swallowed it, head first.

'Very clever,' said the moorhen, admiringly. 'I wish I could do that.'

'Do you happen to know of a good hole in the bank of this pond where I could nest?' asked the kingfisher. 'This seems to be a fine pond for fish. It would be a good place to bring up my young ones. I have a beautiful little wife and we are looking for a place to nest in.'

'Yes!' said the moorhen, eagerly. 'There is a fine hole in the bank over by the hedgerow there, at the end of the pond. It once belonged to a water-vole. Would that do, do you think?'

The kingfisher flew down to the hole and went inside. He soon came out, excited and pleased.

'Just the thing!' he cried. 'I shall fetch my wife and bring her to live here. I am so glad I visited this pond today!'

'Do you know of a little moorhen who would like to come and live with me and build a nest?' called the moorhen.

'I'll see!' said the kingfisher, and off he flew. The next day he was back again with his wife, who was just as brilliant as he was. How excited she was to see the hole in the bank! It did not go quite far enough in, so the two birds busily dug it farther back until they had made a tunnel quite three feet long. It sloped upwards a little to prevent the rain from running in. The moorhen went to see the hole, and the kingfisher told him that he was going to make a nest at the end of it.

'I forgot to tell you something,' he said. 'I saw a moorhen yesterday on the river and she would like to come and live with you. She will soon be here.'

The moorhen was very much excited to hear this. He preened his wings and made them glossy. He swam all round the pond crying 'I shall soon have a wife!' Then he looked carefully for a good place in which to nest.

The little moorhen came the next day. She was a timid little thing, but pretty and good-natured. The moorhen was delighted. He showed her all round the pond and she thought it very comfortable and well stocked with food.

'Here is where I thought we might build our nest,' said the moorhen, showing his mate some thick rushes. She agreed at once. And then, what a happy time they had, the two of them! They were so pleased with one another, so glad to be together in the sunshine! The kingfishers too were very happy. They had made their home in the hole on the bank, and to it they often took the moorhens to show them how comfortable it was. But after a while the moorhens didn't like it. They said it smelt horrible.

So it did! For in the tunnel there were now a great many old fish-bones and fishy pellets that the kingfishers had thrown up after digesting the fish they had eaten. These smelt nasty as they decayed, and the two moorhens could not bear the smell. But the kingfishers didn't mind. Fish was fish whether bad or good, and the smell seemed quite natural to them.

One day the cock-kingfisher called excitedly to the moorhens: 'Kee kee kee! Come and see! We have a nest and eggs now!'

So the moorhens went to see. They peered into the smelly tunnel, and saw the nest at the end – and it was made of old fish-bones! 'What a nest for young ones to hatch on!' thought the cleanly moorhens, in disgust. There were five round eggs, and they gleamed white in the darkness of the tunnel. The mother kingfisher sat down proudly on her eggs again, settling herself comfortably on the fish-bones.

'Come and see *our* nest now!' said the moorhens to the kingfisher. They swam off and the kingfisher followed. Certainly the moorhens' nest was a nice open-air affair after the smelly one in the tunnel. It was a platform made of flattened-out rushes, and it was right on the water itself. In the middle, the platform sank a little to hold the eggs. There were seven eggs there, buff-coloured with red spots, and they were large compared with the kingfishers'.

'It doesn't seem a very *safe* nest to me,' said the kingfisher, doubtfully. 'Why, anyone could see it!'

'But nobody *has*!' said the moorhen as she clambered up to the platform and sat on her eggs.

In the lovely summertime the moorhens' eggs hatched out into amusing little chicks. The kingfishers' eggs hatched too, but nobody saw the young ones for some time, for they were well hidden in the tunnel. Every one knew the moorhens' little black chicks, for before two weeks had passed they were swimming merrily about the pond, seven little black blobs with jerking heads! They followed their father and mother everywhere, and if either of their parents gave the alarm cry and scuttled over the water hurriedly to the reeds, the youngsters would see the white underparts of their parents' tails gleaming brightly and would follow quickly to a safe hiding-place.

Each little bird had a hook-claw on one wing and when they needed to climb up to the platform nest they used this claw as a hand and could reach the nest easily. But one day when they climbed up, what a surprise! There were more eggs in the nest!

'You cannot sleep in the nest now,' said their father. 'I will build you another one nearby. Your mother needs the nest for her second family. You must help her now all you can.'

The little creatures settled happily down on the new nest, and were most excited when the second batch of eggs hatched out. 'Crek! crek!' cried one. 'I will go and find some food for our tiny brothers and sisters!'

Off went all the youngsters eagerly, and soon came back with titbits for the new family. By the next day there were seventeen moorhens – the two parents, seven of the first family, and eight new youngsters, who belonged to the second batch of eggs! How full the pond seemed! What a happy time all the little black moorchicks had, swimming about, calling to one another, bobbing here and there, diving to the bottom, finding food for themselves and the babies – and even helping to make another nest in case their mother laid a third batch of eggs! They were a very happy and contented family.

The chicks were taught many things, and the chief lesson was how to swim underwater to escape an enemy. Their mother was very clever at this. She would bob down under the water and swim across the pond without showing herself at all. Then, at the other side, she would just put her red-marked bill above the water, and nothing else.

All the chicks practised this until they too could swim across the pond under water.

The moorhens were so busy with their two families that they forgot all about the kingfishers – and then one morning, what a surprise! They saw five small kingfishers all sitting on an alder branch over the water, having their first lesson in fishing! The little kingfishers were proud and excited. They had often peeped out of their hole, but they had never fished for themselves before.

'Kee, kee, kee!' called their father, and he dived in to show them how to catch a fish. He flew up to the branch with a gleaming fish in his beak, but he would not give it to any of the hungry youngsters. He threw it back into the pond and it floated there, dead. 'Go and get it if you want it!' cried the kingfisher.

The five small kingfishers looked down hungrily. One of them suddenly opened his wings, dropped down to the water and snatched up the fish. Back to the branch he flew, excited and pleased. He ate the fish and looked down for another.

'Good!' said his father. 'Now try to catch a live fish, or even a fat tadpole. But remember this – knock your fish hard against a branch when you have caught it, for it is unpleasant to swallow a wriggling creature – and *always* swallow it head first, never tail first or it might stick in your throat!'

'But suppose we catch it tail-first,' said a youngster. 'What shall we do?'

'I'll show you!' said the father and he dived in and caught another fish, this time tail first. He knocked it against a branch, threw it up into the air, neatly caught it *head* first and swallowed it! One by one the youngsters dived into the water and soon learnt how to catch fish for themselves. The moorhens enjoyed watching them. And then one day all the kingfishers called goodbye.

'Kee kee kee!' said the old kingfishers. 'There will not be enough food in this small pond for all you moorhens and so many kingfishers. So I am taking my family to the big river where there is more food than a hundred kingfishers can catch. Goodbye! Kee kee kee!'

'Goodbye! Goodbye!' cried all the moorhens at once. The kingfishers flew off, seven bright streaks of blue, and, although the moorhens saw them no more, they often heard them calling to one another from the river. 'Kee kee kee! Kee kee kee!'

THE END

THE WONDERFUL TRAVELLER

In the pond that lay by the alder trees lived a long, strange creature, greenish-brown in colour, with a sharp snout and large eyes. It was a big eel, wise and much travelled, clever at hiding itself in the mud, and sharp at catching unwary fish or newts. Summer and winter it lived in the pond, sometimes leaving it to go for a short journey along the bottom of the ditch when it was muddy and wet. At the sight of the long, thick creature wriggling along, the frogs and toads froze with terror, for it was seldom that they saw the eel in their ditch.

The old toad who had lived under the hedgerow and spawned in the pond for many years knew the eel better than any other creature knew him. He had seen him come to the pond years before! The old toad had seen many strange things and watched scores of curious happenings with his bright, coppery eyes. He was the oldest of all the hedgerow creatures, older even than the badger who sometimes came sniffing along the hedge on a warm night. He often sat and remembered all he had seen and heard, his eyes closed and his body squat, looking for all the world like a lump of earth!

It was while the toad was in the pond with his mate that he saw the eel again. First he saw a mist of mud rise up in the water near a big stone at the bottom. The toad knew that this meant some creature was under the stone, and he swam hurriedly to another stone he knew, and crept under it with his mate. As he watched from his hiding-place he saw the eel wriggle out from under his big stone and dart at an unwary frog. A little water-vole, whose home had an entrance under the water not far from the toad's hiding-place, called out to the toad:

'That's the end of that frog! He was always foolish! He was nearly eaten last week by the duck, and yesterday the heron nearly caught him. Now he is quite gone.'

'Only the strongest or wisest of us live a long life,' said the toad, blinking his eyes. 'I am very old.'

'Are you older than the eel?' asked the water-vole.

'I was here when he came,' said the toad. 'But he was different then. He was much smaller, and his snout was broad, not sharp. His eyes were smaller too. He was not nearly so long as he is now, nor so thick in the body – but that was six years ago! I have watched him change and grow. He came here one spring morning. I remember it quite well.'

'Tell me about it,' begged the little water-vole, who dearly loved a good story.

'I had finished spawning that year,' said the toad, shutting his eyes and trying to remember everything. 'I was squatting on the hedge bank in a rain shower, enjoying the drops on my back, not far from my stone there. I suddenly heard a strange noise in the ditch below.'

55

'What was it?' asked the water-vole.

'I looked down,' said the toad. 'It wasn't a shuffling hedgehog. It wasn't a leaping frog. It wasn't a sliding snake. It was – the eel!'

'Where had he come from?' asked the water-vole in surprise.

'I don't know,' said the toad. 'He just appeared from somewhere. He wriggled along the damp ditch and I followed him on the bank above, for I had never seen an eel before. He came at last to the pond and slid into it. He was only a little creature then, thin and half-transparent. But, as you see, he has grown long and strong, and is an enemy to all small creatures who live in or near the water. He has never found a wife, and has never laid any eggs or had young ones. He is a strange, lonely creature.'

Just then the eel swam up to the toad's stone, and at once the water-vole disappeared into his hole in a great hurry. The toad did not move. He knew that the eel could not reach him, so he sat and looked at the long creature, marvelling at his great length.

'I heard what you said to the vole,' said the eel. 'You do not know everything, old toad. You are right when you say that I am a strange creature, but even you, wise though you are, could not even begin to guess the strange and wonderful life I have led, the long journeys I have made, and the long travels I have still to make! You are an old stay-at-home – I have travelled halfway across the world, and I shall do so again!'

The toad did not believe the eel.

'You are a boaster,' he said. 'You are like the frogs. They say they have been to the moon and back when they see it shining in a puddle!'

The eel was angry. It lashed its long tail and made little waves on the top of the pond.

'Listen to me,' it said. 'I was born thousands of miles away in the depths of an ocean.'

'What is an ocean?' asked the toad in surprise. 'Is it like this pond?'

'It is endless water!' said the eel. 'It is deep, so deep, and there are thousands of weird and marvellous creatures living in its depths, besides many beautiful fish. I have seen them all. I hatched out of an egg nine years ago, so I am old, very old. I was a strange-looking creature then, and knew little.'

'What were you like?' asked the toad, curiously.

'I was leaf-like in shape,' said the eel, trying to remember, 'and very thin – as thin as that sheet of brown paper that once lay by the pond-side. I am as long and round as a pipe now, I know, but in those days I was flat and you could have seen right through me, for I was transparent. I swam about for a while in the deep ocean and then I and many many thousands of other silvery eels began to swim to the north-east – and after about three years I came to the land! I had changed on the way. I became smaller, and my body lost its flat shape and became rounder as it is now.'

'What did you do next?' asked the toad, his eyes nearly bulging out of his head with wonder at this strange story.

'I left the sea and swam up a big river,' said the eel. 'Many other eels were with me. We swam up in a great shoal. Then gradually our company broke up. Some entered small streams. Some swam to a lake. I found the ditch out there by the hedgerow. It was full of water then from the spring rains, and it led me to this pond. Here I have been ever since, growing bigger and longer each year. Ah, you should have seen us on that long journey toad! Once we came to a lock-gate, and it was shut – so we scrambled over it! And another time we came to a rushing waterfall, which, every time we tried to clamber up, knocked us down again. So we wriggled our way up the old moss-grown stones by the side of the waterfall. It was a great adventure.'

'Shall you stay here always?' asked the toad. 'What will happen if you grow bigger and bigger and bigger? The pond will not hold you!' 'The time is nearly come when I must go again,' said the eel. 'I felt last December that I must go, for the ditches then were moist and easy to journey through, and the streams were full and rushed to the sea – so I started out, but I was caught in an eel-trap and hurt my back. Then I came back here again to my pond to get better. But now I must soon go, for I have lost my greenish-brown colouring and have become silvery. All eels must go back to the sea when they become old. They must find wives and must lay their eggs in the deep ocean so that there may be thousands of other young eels to follow them. It will take me many months to reach my birthplace and I must go before I die.'

'Well, your tale is wonderful,' said the toad, his throat swelling with a loud croak. 'But I shall not be sorry to say goodbye to you, eel, for you have many a time tried to catch me, and you must have eaten hundreds of toads in your life.'

'I would not eat a wise old toad like you,' promised the eel.

'You might not know it was I until you had swallowed me,' said the toad, wisely, quite determined not to move from his safe hiding-place.

Suddenly the eel twisted his head round and stared in amazement at a small creature which had just wriggled up to him. The toad stretched out his head to have a look. He saw another eel – but very, very small indeed.

'Where do you come from?' cried the large eel in delight and amazement.

'From the deep seas,' answered the small creature, who was so transparent that he looked as if he might almost be made of glass. 'I was born there, as you were, cousin. It has taken me three years and more to get to this pond. Is there good hunting here?'

'Plenty of everything,' answered the eel, swimming round his small cousin in delight. 'See how I have grown here. I am surely the biggest eel you have met in your journeys.'

'Oh no, I have met far bigger eels than you,' said the small eel. 'Why did you not leave your pond earlier, cousin? You are old, and you should not leave your last journey till you are weak, for it is a very long way. You may die before you get to our birthplace.'

'I shall go this very day,' said the big eel. 'Most of the old eels went in the autumn, I know, but we have had much rain lately, and the streams are full of water. It will be easy for me to swim down with the current, and I shall soon reach the sea.'

'Beware of eel-traps, cousin,' warned the small eel. 'We elvers escaped them, for we are very small – but you are big.'

The eel called goodbye to the little elver and swam to the ditch that led into the pond. He wriggled into it and saw the old toad sitting high up on the bank, watching.

'Goodbye!' cried the eel. 'I go on my long journey back to the depths of the ocean again.'

'You are a wonderful traveller!' called back the toad. 'Goodbye! It is a pity you cannot take your small cousin with you. He will be just as much danger to us when he grows, as *you* have been. Goodbye – and good riddance!'

But the eel did not hear. He had left the pond and the hedgerow behind him for ever.

THE END